INIQUITY

A FABLE FROM THE DEAD ISSUE SCROLL

BY SABREPEN

THOMAS NELSON INC., PUBLISHERS

NASHVILLE·CAMDEN·NEW YORK

COPYRIGHT © 1974 BY
THOMAS NELSON, INC.
ALL RIGHTS RESERVED
UNDER INTERNATIONAL AND
PAN-AMERICAN CONVENTIONS.
PUBLISHED BY THOMAS NELSON,
INC., NASHVILLE, TENNESSEE.

ISBN 8407-4039-5

MANUFACTURED IN THE UNITED
STATES OF AMERICA.

TO THE REMNANTS
   OF CIVILIZATION
IN THE GREAT SOCIETY.

ONTENTS

PART I 11
(IN WHICH **HE** RESIGNS)

PART II 45
(THE CONSEQUENCES
OF THE "EXPECTATION")

PART III 77
(THE "ANSWER")

ABOUT THIS FABLE 95

A Fable

FROM THE AGE OF UNIVERSAL HARMONY

PART I

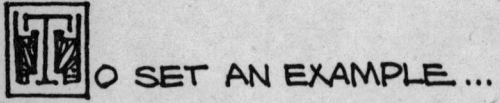O SET AN EXAMPLE....

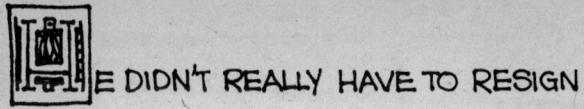
HE DIDN'T REALLY HAVE TO RESIGN.

NO ONE COULD HAVE FORCED HIM.

NOR DID HE REALLY WANT TO RESIGN.

But he did so.

'ELUCTANTLY AND REGRETFULLY..."
SO HE SAID, CLAIMING THAT THOSE WHO LED THE DEMAND HAD, BY THEIR METHODS, MADE IT IMPOSSIBLE FOR HIM TO OTHERWISE DO FURTHER SERVICE FOR THE COUNTRY.

O...,

TO SET AN EXAMPLE...,

HE...

RESIGNED...

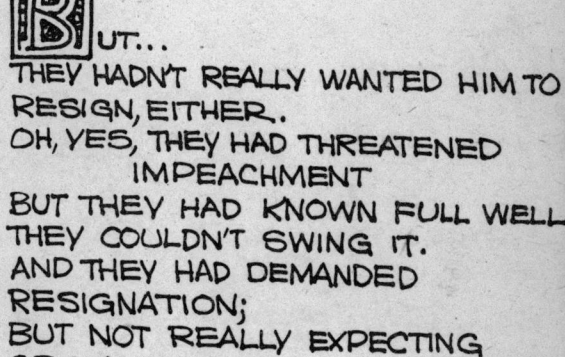

But...
they hadn't really wanted him to resign, either.
Oh, yes, they had threatened
 IMPEACHMENT
but they had known full well they couldn't swing it.
And they had demanded resignation;
but not really expecting or wanting it.

THEIR PURPOSES...APPARENTLY NOT RECOGNIZED BY MOST OF THEIR CLAMOROUS FOLLOWING... COULD BE SEEN IN THE PATTERN OF EVENTS LEADING UP TO THE UNEXPECTED GRAND FINALE OF ACTUAL RESIGNATION...

FIRST, SEVERAL RUMORS AND COMPLAINTS ABOUT HIM WERE HEADLINE NEWS.

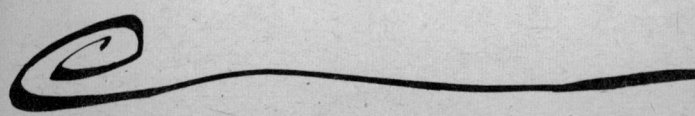

ny real
  or
    imagined
      misdeeds
of persons even remotely
associated with him being used
to lend credence to the
coming inundation.

Including over enthusiastic
campaign workers and a
gardener who claimed too
much tax deduction for the
    gasoline in
      his Roto-Tiller©!

Quickly, opinion pollsters reported that his popularity was falling. Columnists declared that his failure to answer all questions raised by themselves was causing distrust and disunity amongst the people.

"HE SHOULD BE PUT OUT OF OFFICE!"... Newscasters reported high placed sources as saying. And the cry "PUT HIM OUT!" was echoed by many TV watchers who thought that, by listening to those newscasts, they must surely be
   FULLY
    INFORMED.

"HE SHOULD BE IMPEACHED!"
THE COMMENTATORS DECIDED.
"IMPEACH! IMPEACH!"
CAME THE CRIES...AND BUMPER
STICKERS...IN RESPONSE.

"E OUGHT TO RESIGN!" ONE LEADER OF THOUGHT DECLARED. (AND EVEN A FEW FRIENDS...) AND THE RESPONDING CHORUS QUICKLY ADJUSTED ITS REFRAIN ACCORDINGLY.

IN VARIED TONES, THAT REFRAIN REVERBERATED ACROSS THE LAND. FROM PULPITS... AND FROM POOL HALLS. FROM HOUSES OF DISTINCTION... AND FROM HOUSES OF ILL REPUTE. IN CIVIC CLUB LUNCHEONS AND IN PROFESSIONAL GATHERINGS (WHERE ETHICS AND MORALITY ARE...

ALWAYS
OF PRIME CONCERN).
SOME WORKERS HUMMED IT
ON THE JOB. WELFARISTS JIVED
IT UP WHILE WAITING FOR ONE
HANDOUT OR WHILE DEMANDING
ANOTHER.

COLLEGE PROFESSORS COMPETED WITH STUDENTS TO COME UP WITH THE MOST ERUDITE PROFUNDITIES. IN HIGH SCHOOLS, WHERE THERE IS USUALLY MORE DECORUM, IT WAS THE SUBJECT OF CURRENT EVENTS DISCUSSIONS.

HICH WAS EXACTLY THE KIND OF PUBLIC REACTION THE ORCHESTRA LEADERS WANTED. IF THE CONCERT COULD BE KEPT UP UNTIL THE NEXT ELECTIONS, HOW COULD THEIR CANDIDATES POSSIBLY LOSE? (NO MATTER THAT THE CRESCENDO WAS DUE MORE TO AMPLIFICATION THAN TO INCREASED MEMBERSHIP IN THE CHOIR.)

Now, suddenly, his actual resignation had wiped out the "big issue" on which his political enemies were counting for the next elections. However, this was of no real importance because popular reaction to his formal statement of resignation wiped out the next elections.

That formal statement was quite brief. He neither denied nor confirmed the accusations his critics had made. He acknowledged no obligation to tell everything about everything he had ever done.

He was resigning, he said, "in the interests of harmony" and "to set an example" for all his countrymen.

He asked nothing for himself ... of anyone.
    But
        He
           Did
              Express
                  An...

Expectation"...

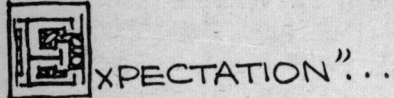

"I DO EXPECT," HE SAID, "BECAUSE BY THE POSTULATES OF MY CRITICS I AM COMPELLED TO EXPECT IT, THAT EVERY ONE OF MY FELLOW CITIZENS... MOST ESPECIALLY THOSE IN POSITIONS OF PUBLIC TRUST, OR AUTHORITY, OR INFLUENCE... WHO HAS EVER BEEN EVEN
     SUSPECTED
         OF FALLING SHORT
OF HIS DUTIES, OR OF VIOLATING HIS PROFESSED CODE,... ALSO
        WILL
           RESIGN
ONLY THEN CAN WE HAVE UNIVERSAL HARMONY."

NATURALLY,
NO ONE
COULD REFUSE TO FOLLOW
SUCH A SELFLESS
AND NOBLE EXAMPLE
AS THAT...

And so it came to pass that the world entered into what was called, "The Age of Universal Harmony."

ONLY, AT FIRST, IT WASN'T ENTIRELY HARMONIOUS. IN FACT, QUITE FRANKLY, IT WAS CACOPHONOUS

THE FIRST DAY A.R. (AFTER RESIGNATION) WAS CHAOTIC. CHILDREN ARRIVING AT SCHOOL FOUND THAT THEIR TEACHERS "IN THE INTEREST OF HARMONY" HAD RESIGNED.

And some children returned home to find that mom and dad had resigned their parenthoods for the same reason.

OFFICE BUILDINGS IN EVERY CITY WERE DESERTED... EXCEPT FOR MAYBE A JANITOR OR TWO. THIS INCLUDED GOVERNMENT OFFICES, CHAMBERS OF THE NATIONAL LEGISLATURE BEING THE FIRST FULLY VACATED... EXCEPT FOR A JANITOR OR TWO.

NO ONE GAVE A THOUGHT TO NAMING A REPLACEMENT, BECAUSE NO ONE FELT QUALIFIED EVEN TO THINK ABOUT THAT... EXCEPT MAYBE A JANITOR OR TWO. AS FOR ACTUALLY FINDING A REPLACEMENT, UNDER THE TERMS OF THE "EXPECTATION" NO ONE COULD POSSIBLY QUALIFY, ANYWAY ... EXCEPT FOR A JANITOR OR TWO. AND THE JANITORS WERE ALL TOO BUSY CLEANING UP THE MESS LEFT BY RESIGNED AND HASTILY DEPARTED LEGISLATORS AND BUREAUCRATS.

A JUNIOR LEGISLATOR WHO HAD B.R. (BEFORE RESIGNATION) CALLED FOR "FULL DISCLOSURE" BY ALL PUBLIC OFFICIALS, SCUTTLED OFF TO HIS SECLUDED SEASHORE ESTATE, THEREAFTER SPENDING MOST OF HIS TIME SKIN DIVING IN NEARBY BAYS AND INLETS. ANOTHER RESIGNEE, NOTING HIM DIVING REPEATEDLY IN THE SAME SPOT, ASKED (MERELY FOR THE SAKE OF CONVERSATION, OF COURSE) IF HE WERE LOOKING FOR SOMETHING IN PARTICULAR. SOMEWHAT VEXEDLY CAME THE REPLY! "OWUH LEADUH DIDN'T TELL ALL ON HIM WHEN HE RESIGNED, SO I DON'T HAVE TO TELL ALL ON ME."

A SENIOR LEGISLATOR WHO HAD SAID B.R. (BEFORE RESIGNATION) THAT THE TOP OFFICIAL WAS EVER OBLIGATED TO "SET A PERSONAL EXAMPLE IN ALL WAYS FOR THE REST OF US TO FOLLOW" SHUFFLED BACK TO THE HILLS OF HIS CHILDHOOD AND WROTE A SCHOLARLY BUT NEVER PUBLISHED OPUS, "THE ESSENTIALITY OF INCONSISTENCY TO SUCCESSFUL POLITICKING." TO OTHER MEMBERS OF THE SPIT 'N WHITTLE CLUB HE CONFIDED HIS BELIEF THAT "ONLY BECAUSE OUR LEADER SET A BAD EXAMPLE BY RESIGNING," WERE THERE NO PUBLISHERS STILL IN BUSINESS WHO WOULD CONSIDER HIS MANUSCRIPT.

ANOTHER LEGISLATOR... WHO HAD BEEN AN "ALSO-RAN" IN A PREVIOUS RACE FOR THE TOP JOB... SOUGHT OUT A RETIRED CHIEF ON AN INDIAN RESERVATION AND BEGGED THE CHIEF TO REACTIVATE THE TRIBE SO THAT HE MIGHT JOIN AS AN APPRENTICE BRAVE.

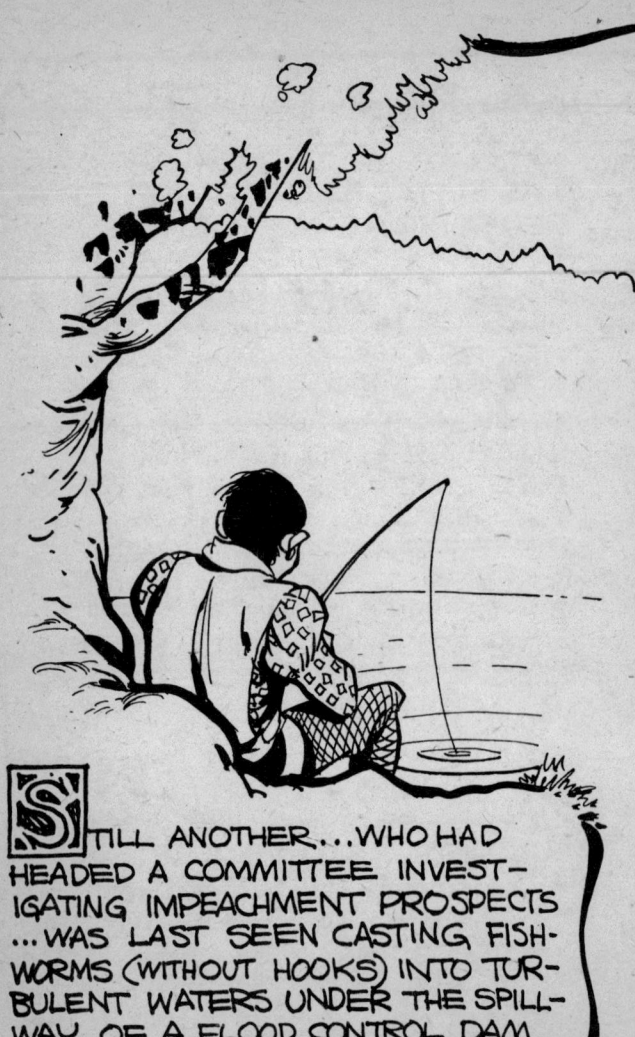

Still another...who had headed a committee investigating impeachment prospects ...was last seen casting fishworms (without hooks) into turbulent waters under the spillway of a flood control dam.

An ex-bureaucrat, who had once investigated some of the accusations, gave up a lucrative private law practice and applied for a job as janitor in the Justice Department.

And a judge, who had been hearing "evidence" in the whole affair, spent the rest of his days listening for flaws in his home hi-fi recordings.

THE STREETS TEEMED WITH RESIGNEES. AT FIRST THEY WERE ELATED BY THE FEELING OF HAVING "DONE RIGHT BY THE COUNTRY" IN FOLLOWING THE LEADER. BUT THEY SOON GREW RESTLESS, SEEKING PLACES TO WHILE AWAY THE HOURS THEY HAD PREVIOUSLY WHILED AWAY AT THEIR JOBS.

SHOPPING WAS DIFFICULT. THE ONLY SHOPS STILL OPEN WERE THOSE WHOSE OWNERS HAD NEVER MISREPRESENTED THE QUALITY OF THEIR WARES... OR THE TERMS OF THEIR CREDIT SALES. BESIDES, ALL GOODS HAD BEEN TAKEN OFF THE MARKET WHOSE MAKERS HAD EVER SO MUCH AS EXAGGERATED THE MERITS OF THEIR PRODUCTS.

The restless resignee who went for a drive, now found (in addition to the "OUT-OF-GAS" signs due to the shortage) many service stations closed by resignation of owners or managers. The only stations still in business were those who had
    NEVER
       DONE
         SUCH
           THINGS
as sell a short gallon or hike tow truck prices during a snowstorm.

Worse still, if one had mechanical trouble, any unresigned repairman would be at the far end of a long waiting
      LINE—.

SICK PEOPLE, IF THEY COULD FIND AN UNRESIGNED DOCTOR TO WRITE A PRESCRIPTION, HAD THEN TO FIND AN UNRESIGNED DRUGGIST TO FILL IT.

THE ACUTE SHORTAGE OF UNRESIGNED POLICEMEN, JUDGES, AND LAWYERS WAS FRIGHTENING... UNTIL IT BECAME EVIDENT THAT THIS SHORTAGE OF LAW ENFORCERS AND LEGAL ADVISERS WAS MORE THAN OFFSET BY A COMPLETE ABSENCE OF ROBBERIES, ASSAULTS, RAPES, MURDERS, AND OTHER ANTI-SOCIAL ACTIVITIES; ALL MISCREANTS HAVING RESIGNED FROM COMMITTING MISCREANCIES. (EVERY CLOUD MUST HAVE A SILVER LINING... AT LEAST, A LITTLE BIT.)

Despairing in their quest for other pastimes, resignees began retreating to their homes. If the local power company was still in business, they could watch TV.

But many of their favorite programs were now un-cast. The commentator who had first called for the leader's resignation was also first to announce his own. He was quickly followed by all the other newscasters who had ever allowed their castings to be influenced by their personal opinions.

Adding to these 'withdrawal miseries' for the TV addict, a weak tube could now spell total disaster. TV repairmen of any sort had been hard to get B.R. (Before Resignation). Now, A.R. (After Resignation), one's fingers might be worn out from walking through the yellow pages and dialing just to get on the waiting list of a serviceman who had never in some manner overcharged or oversold on a house call. And, if something went wrong with the beer cooler or the plumbing, trying to find an unresigned electrician or plumber was... forget it!

Newspapers were no substitute. Minus the "come-on" ads of businesses no longer in business, and without "interpretative reports" or commentary on impeachment or resignation, the once-mammoth big city dailies weren't even big enough to

       WRAP
         UP
          THE
           HOUSEHOLD
            GARBAGE.

First reactions of resignees to these frustrations were generally passive. Some just sat,
   resignedly,
      in front of their dead TV's and imagined they were seeing a re-run of 'Fantasia' or perhaps a game between Saints and Dolphins.

Others sat at the wheels of their gasless autos, purring engine noises and imagining a leisurely drive on a parkway, or beating the pack from a signal, or, nostalgically, fighting rush hour traffic back to the job from which they had resigned.

SHEER BOREDOM SOON BEGAN TO DRIVE THEM BACK OUT OF THEIR HOUSES TO MEANDER ABOUT THE NEIGHBORHOOD.

SOME MIGHT WANDER PAST A CHURCH; BUT THE IMPULSE TO ENTER WOULD LIKELY AS NOT BE SNUFFED OUT BY A NOTE OF RESIGNATION LEFT ON THE DOOR BY MINISTER, PRIEST, OR RABBI (AS THE CASE MIGHT BE), OFTEN ACCOMPANIED BY SIMILAR NOTES FROM ORGANIST, CHOIR DIRECTOR... OR EVEN A PILLAR OR TWO.

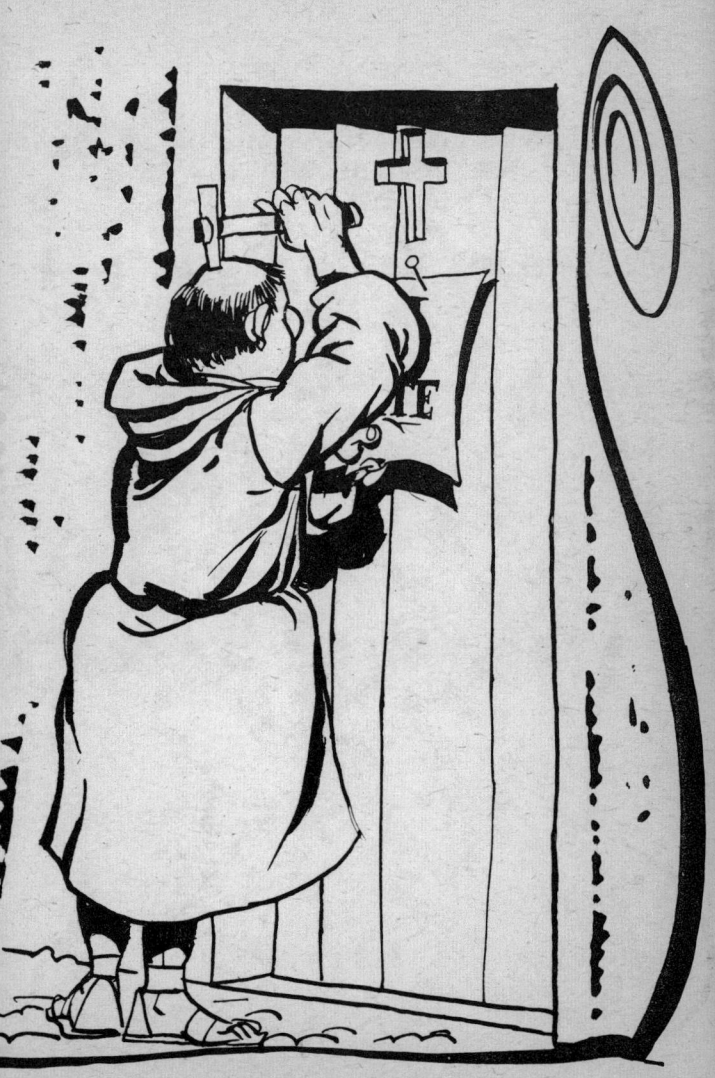

ND SO IT WENT THROUGHOUT THE LAND...
EVERYWHERE A
RESIGNEE WENT
HE RAN
SMACK-DAB INTO
SOMEBODY ELSE'S RESIGNATION!

SOME CYNICS WOULD EVEN REFER TO THE TIMES AS THE "AGE OF RESIGNATION." BUT, OFFICIALLY, IT WAS THE "AGE OF HARMONY" BECAUSE THAT IS WHAT IT WAS LABELLED WHILE THERE WAS STILL SOMEBODY IN OFFICE WITH AUTHORITY TO LABEL ANYTHING.

THE NEAREST THING TO COMPLETE HARMONY CAME ABOUT WHEN ALL COMMERCE HAD STOPPED; WHEN EVEN THOSE WHO DIDN'T HAVE TO RESIGN TO FULFILL THE "EXPECTATION" DID SO BECAUSE THEY COULD FIND NO ONE ELSE UNRESIGNED TO DO BUSINESS WITH.

THE WHEELS OF THE NATION'S INDUSTRIES ALL HAD STOPPED. THERE WERE NO TRAFFIC NOISES. NO JACKHAMMERS. NO CHURCH BELL OR SCHOOL BUZZERS. HARDLY ANY SOUNDS AT ALL EXCEPT A LOW HUM OF GRUMBLE FROM THE MULTITUDE OF RESIGNED PEOPLE MILLING ABOUT WITH NOTHING ELSE TO DO AND, FOR THE MOST PART, NOT ENOUGH LIFE LEFT IN THEM TO DO ANYTHING ELSE, ANYWAY.

NEAR TOTAL HARMONY, BUT NOT QUITE.

NOW AND AGAIN THERE WOULD ARISE FROM THE HUM A LONE CRY OR SHRIEK, FROM SOME FEARFUL OR DESPAIRING SOUL SUDDENLY INFUSED BY A LAST GASP OF HUMAN SPIRIT.

SOMETIMES THESE WERE CURSES... AT THE CROWD, GENERALLY, OR AT THE CIRCUMSTANCE; SOMETIMES DAMNING THE RESIGNED LEADER AS CAUSE OF THE CIRCUMSTANCE BECAUSE HE RESIGNED.

OFTEN THEY WERE GIBBERISH, OR JUST LOUD NOISES. BUT ALWAYS THEY RECEDED BACK INTO THAT OTHERWISE 'HARMONIOUS' HUM OF GRUMBLE FROM WHICH THEY AROSE.

UNTIL...PERHAPS UNTHINKINGLY ...A LOUD AND CLARION VOICE RANG OUT TO ASK:

"OH, LORD, WHAT SHALL WE DO?"

THEN A GREAT HUSH FELL UPON THE MULTITUDE... AS THOUGH EVERY SOUL WITHIN IT HAD ASKED THE QUESTION AND NOW AWAITED AN ANSWER. FOR A FEW MOMENTS, WHICH HUNG AS ETERNITY, NOTHING SEEMED TO BE HAPPENING—.

THEN THE SKY BEGAN NOTICE-
ABLY TO
DARKEN.

Except for an occasional gasp of hope or trepidation, the multitude remained silent for several minutes. As darkness deepened, however, new sounds of fear began to arise. And when the darkness was nearly total, there was much weeping, wailing, and gnashing of teeth.

SUDDENLY THE SCENE WAS ILLUMINED BY BRILLIANT FLASHES OF LIGHTNING STRIKING REPEATEDLY ON A DISTANT MOUNTAIN.

Full silence gripped the multitude again as they watched, entranced, a most awesome display of nature's force. Their entrancement continued even after the lightning stopped as suddenly as it had begun and the sky cleared quickly to a gentle blue.

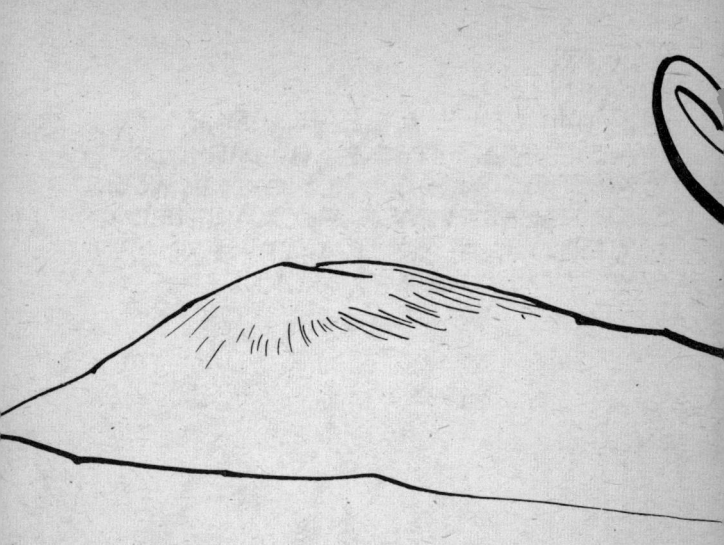

Then, slowly, as they emerged from the trance, it seemed to dawn on the people that what they had just seen must have been in response to that last plaintive cry which had arisen from their midst.

In which case, it would logically follow, the answer to that question might very well now be graven in the rock of yon distant mountain.

QUICKLY A SEARCH PARTY ASSEMBLED ITSELF... BY IMPULSE AND INSTINCT, SINCE NO ONE WOULD PRESUME HIMSELF QUALIFIED TO ORGANIZE OR LEAD IT... AND SET OUT TO THE MOUNTAIN.

Many long hours they traveled... up ever-steepening slopes...

ALONG NARROW LEDGES THEY CREPT, EVER HIGHER... SCALING NEAR-VERTICAL CLIFFS... CROSSING TREACHEROUS SLIDES AND CREVASSES... PERFORMING FEATS OF STRENGTH AND ENDURANCE OF WHICH ONLY DESPERATE MEN (AND DESPERATE LIBERATED WOMEN, OF COURSE) ARE SAID TO BE CAPABLE!

THROUGH A THICK CLOUD-FOG THEY GROPED THEIR WAY STILL HIGHER, FINALLY EMERGING IN BRILLIANT SUNLIGHT UPON A HIGH PLATEAU. AND, AT ONCE, THEY ALL SAW IT!

SHARPLY ENGRAVED ON A SHEER WHITE CLIFF, INACCESSIBLE BECAUSE OF A DEEP GORGE BEFORE THEM, THESE WERE THE SIMPLE WORDS:

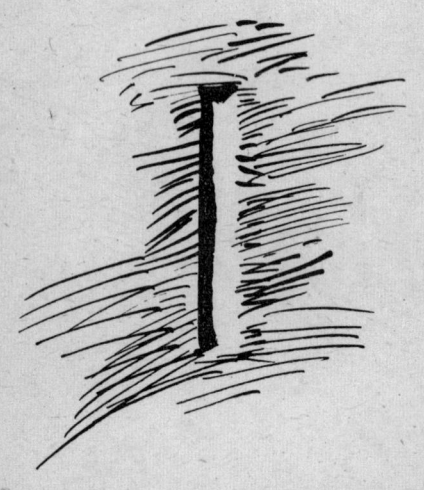

When I first discovered this fable in a remote spot in the Blue Ridge Mountains of Virginia, it bore the date "Dec. '73." But how can one know for certain which of the twenty "73's" that have passed on our calendar this notation signifies? That's the trouble with fables, anyhow. It's so hard to pinpoint just when and to whom they apply.

Because "Blue Ridge Mountain Cavern Scroll" seems a bit unwieldy, I elected to call my discovery the "Dead Issue Scroll" bearing in mind that continued beating on the carcass did not restore life to the horse in that old adage.

No doubt some will view this work as a defense of Nixon simply because it isn't another stone thrown at him. But it is my contention that the renowned expression about "who is not for me is against me" really applies to only one Being. And toward all other mortals, including myself, there is much occasion for a neutral, a detached, or a "wait and see" attitude.

Some may consider it irreverent, but I'm confident that our good Lord who bore the mantle of suspicion and accusation with the supreme degree of courage, has more than a sufficient sense of humor to tolerate this.

In every age or era, politics has been more or less a joke. Perhaps it's time we laughed a little... through our tears.

Sabrepen

Sabrepen

Have thoughts will travel